A Perfect Fit!

and other stories

Short Story Anthology 1

STARTERS

First published 2001
Revised edition 2005

The Educational Company of Ireland
Ballymount Road
Walkinstown
Dublin 12

A member of the Smurfit Kappa Group

© For this anthology – Aidan Herron, Anne Marie Herron, Jane Kelly,
Dolores O'Donnell

Illustrations: Michael Connor, Brian Fitzgerald, Maria Murray, Bill
Piggins, Oksana Popova, Kim Shaw, Margaret Anne Suggs,
Kate Walsh, Annie West

Design and layout: Graham & Stapleton Design Consultants

Printed in the Republic of Ireland by DCK.

Aen 2361P

3456789

Acknowledgements
- 'Show and Tell' from *Unusual Day* – Sandi Toksvig, Corgi Pups.
  Reprinted by permission of The Random House Group Ltd.
- 'The Terrible Monster Jelly' from *Badjelly the Witch and Dip the
  Puppy* – Spike Milligan, a Target Book.
- 'Such a Fuss!' from *I'm Bored!* – Bel Mooney, Mammoth.
- 'Dear Mum and Dad' from *Little Wolf's Book of Badness* – Ian
  Whybrow, Collins.
- 'Collector Mania' from *The Crazy Collector* – Diana Hendry,
  Barrington Stoke.
- 'The Turtle and the Crane' from *Our Favourite Stories from Around
  the World* – as told by Wendy Body, The Book Project, Longman.
- 'A Day in the Life of a Killer Cat' from *The Diary of A Killer Cat* –
  Anne Fine, (Hamish Hamilton, 1994) © Anne Fine, 1994.
- 'A Perfect Fit!' from *Too Big!* – Geraldine McCaughrean, Corgi Pubs.

*In the case of some copyright pieces, the publishers have been unable to
contact the copyright holders but will be glad to make the appropriate
arrangements with them as soon as they make contact.*

Contents

Show and Tell

Sandi Toksvig

The children in Blue Class were used to bringing things to school to put on show. They loved seeing what everybody brought in on 'Nature day' and on 'Pet Day'. Then teacher said they were going to have an 'Unusual Day'. What could Jessica bring?

Blue Class were having an 'Unusual Day'. Well, there was nothing unusual about the day itself. Everyone had been to assembly as usual, everyone had done quiet reading as usual and everyone had drunk their juice in break as usual. It was after lunch that the unusual part was to happen.

All the children had been asked to bring in something 'unusual' to talk about. The idea had started with Blue Class having a 'Blue Day' where everyone had to bring in something blue.

Then they had a 'Nature Day' where

everyone had to bring something from the garden, followed by 'Pet Day'. 'Pet Day' had not been entirely successful. All the dogs, cats and hamsters had behaved very well, but Kristian's snake had gone missing. The classroom had been turned upside down looking for Barry the Boa.

The snake finally turned up ten minutes before the bell in the Rainy Day Box. Mrs Robinson, who played piano on Tuesdays, had found him. It was a shame Barry had given her such a fright, but everyone had had such fun playing hospital while they waited for her to come round. Blue Class's teacher, Miss Johnson, who has very red hair and is in charge, says there won't be music on Tuesdays this term.

Today, however, was 'Unusual Day'. Miss Johnson had told the children they could bring in anything that was really different. Joey had brought a doll from Russia called a 'Babushka'.

It was made of brightly painted wood and

 had lots of other dolls inside it. Kristian had brought a nappy from his baby sister. She had worn it all night and it was still dry. His mother had said it was 'most unusual'. Esme, who had been

a big hit on 'Nature Day' with her slug collection, had found a four-leafed clover.

As they arrived, everyone had put their  unusual things on the big table so that Miss Johnson could label them. Jessica Grace was late.

'Hello Jessica,' said Miss Johnson, putting someone's three-legged *My Little Pony* at the back of the table. 'Have you brought something unusual today?'

'Yes,' said Jessica. 'She's outside.'

'She?' asked Miss Johnson.

Jessica nodded. 'I've brought my granny.'

Extract from *Unusual Day* by Sandi Toksvig, Corgi Pups. Reprinted by permission of The Random House Group Ltd.

The Terrible Monster Jelly
Spike Milligan

What is your favourite dessert? The King in this story loves jelly so much that he cannot get enough. The greedy King gets a big surprise when Peepo and Maria's daddy brings him The Terrible Monster Jelly!

Once upon a time, a hundred and wobbly years ago, in a town called Mdina, on the island of Malta, there lived a family: a mummy and daddy and two children, a boy called Peepo and a girl called Maria. The town was surrounded by big fortress walls so no one could get in except through the one big main gate. Outside of the town lived lots of families who all worked on farms. The farms belonged to a wicked and cruel King who lived in a palace in Mdina. He made all the farmers and their children work very hard from early in the morning to late at night. He only gave them a little money, and if

any of them became sick, he would not let them
see a doctor, or go to bed, and sometimes the
sick people died. So all the mummys, daddys
and their children were very sad and very
hungry. The King had plenty of money and
food, and he was very greedy; Peepo and
Maria's daddy worked as a cook in the King's
kitchen. He was a very good cook and could
make lovely cakes and puddings and bright
coloured jellies, but the King was always cruel
to the daddy. The King would say, 'This jelly is
too small. I want a bigger one,' and he would

throw the jelly on the floor, where his dogs would eat it all up. So the poor daddy would go back to the kitchen and make a bigger jelly, and then the King would eat it all up and say, 'I'm still hungry. Make a bigger one quickly, or I will chop your head off.' The poor daddy worked all night and made a jelly as big as a chair, but the wicked King ate it all up, *'Gibble, Gobble, Gibble, Gobble, Swallow, Swallow, Glup!'*

Then he said, 'I'm still hungry. If by tomorrow evening you haven't made me a bigger jelly, I will put both your children in a dark underground prison till they die!' When the daddy went home and told the family they were all very frightened and the mummy started to cry. The daddy said, 'I don't know how to make a bigger jelly.' When the children went to bed they said prayers, 'Please, God, help us to stop the wicked King from putting us in prison.' Then they went to sleep.

Early in the morning when it was still asleep-time there was a tap-tappity-tap on the window. 'Wake up!' said Maria to Peepo. They got up and went to the window, and there outside was a beautiful little angel-fairy.

She was only as big as a thimble and she was holding a tiny jelly on a plate. The children opened the window and let her in. 'Who are you?' said the children. 'I am Saint Chivers. God heard you praying for help and He sent me with this jelly for the King.' 'That's too small for the wicked King,' said Peepo. 'He wants a giant jelly.'

'Don't worry,' said Saint Chivers, 'this is a magic jelly. You keep it and give it to the King tomorrow and you will see how it is a magic jelly,' and the angel-fairy flew away. The children went back to sleep. When they woke up again they saw that the little jelly had got bigger. 'Oh, we'll have to put it on a bigger plate,' they said. They rushed downstairs and told their mummy and daddy about the magic jelly and what the angel-fairy had said. They all ran upstairs with a bigger plate but the jelly had got too big for the second plate. So they took the magic jelly downstairs and put it on a bigger plate. But it was still getting bigger and bigger, so the daddy said, 'I'll put it in a big bucket.'

When he had done this he ran to the King's palace, and the jelly was bigger still, so he put it on a big round table. The King was shouting, 'Hurry up! I want my jelly.' The jelly was now as big as a window and the daddy had to get three men to help him carry the magic jelly to the King's dinner table. When the King saw the jelly it was as high as a door, but even then he wasn't satisfied. 'It's still too small. As soon as I've eaten it up, with a Gobbledy Glup, I'm going to throw you, your wife, and your children into a deep dark prison full of snakes and mud!' Two soldiers grabbed the poor daddy and tied him up. 'Go and bring his wife and children here and tie them up too,' said the wicked King. Then the King started to eat the magic jelly.

'Oh yum-yum-yummummy
I've got jelly in my tummy!'

he said. He sat eating for over one hour. 'That's funny,' said the wicked King, 'the jelly hasn't got smaller.' By now the guards had brought back the two children and their mummy, all tied up with chains. They watched as the King tried to eat all the magic jelly but, no, he couldn't. The jelly was getting bigger and

bigger – and people started to laugh. The King
was so angry! The jelly was now half as big as
the room so they had to take it out to the
garden. Then it got as big as the garden and
the King was still trying to eat it as fast as he
could. '*Eat-Eat-Fast-Eat-Eat,*' he went, but the
jelly got as big as the garden, so they had to
carry it out into the street.

   By now the King had eaten so much jelly he
was as fat as a house. All his trousers had split

open and showed his bare bottom. Everybody
was laughing at him and he was so angry he
started to cry. Still the jelly got bigger and
bigger – so he made the people carry it into the
park, and then he had eaten so much and he
was so full of jelly, his tummy was like a big big
round ball and he fell over and rolled down the

street, through the gate, out into the fields where all the poor people were working. The magic jelly was getting bigger than the park. 'Someone help me,' screamed the King. 'If someone doesn't eat it all, that jelly will fill the whole city and my palace will be inside the jelly.' Just then, the soldiers came down the road with their prisoners and Peepo and Maria said to the King, 'If we get rid of the jelly, will you promise to be kind and give plenty of food to the poor people?'

'Oh yes, I promise,' said the King, 'and I'll never be bad again.' So the soldiers released Peepo and Maria who got all the poor children together and said, 'Who likes jelly?' and all the poor hungry children said, 'We do.' So they all marched to the King's palace; they each got a spoon from the kitchen, and they went to the park and started to eat the giant jelly, and they were so hungry they ate it all up in twenty minutes and three seconds – a world record for eating jellies.

Then they all sang –

'Yuma-Yuma-Yummy
We've got jelly in our tummy
Now we'll all go home
To Daddy and Mummy.'

The King was so pleased he gave each family a hundred gold and silver coins, and all the children a gold spoon with their name on it, and he was never cruel any more, and they all lived happily until the next jelly.

Extract from *Badjelly the Witch and Dip the Puppy* by Spike Milligan, A Target Book

Such a Fuss!

Bel Mooney

Everybody makes such a fuss of a new baby!
Kitty feels a little left out when her baby brother
Thomas is born.

It was four weeks since Baby Thomas was
born, and the house had changed forever.
There were little white blankets, cardigans
and bootees everywhere, and tiny coloured
all-in-one suits hanging on the washing-line.

The pram filled the hall, and the cot took up the space by Mum's bed – where Kitty used to climb in, sometimes, in the mornings. Through the day there would be very noisy times when the baby would cry and cry and cry, until Kitty thought his little red head would cry itself off his shoulders.

Then there would be times when Mum said, 'Shhhh!' and Kitty had to tiptoe around and talk in a whisper. That was very difficult indeed.

The worst thing was that Mum and Dad and Daniel seemed to have gone a bit mad. Kitty would come across one of them hanging over the cot or the pram or the rug on the sitting-room floor where Thomas kicked his legs.

'Whoo's a sweetie? Whoo's Dada's darlin' ickle diddums baby boy, then?' cooed Dad.

'Such a little preshus ... such a boofulbabba,' whispered Mum.

'Helloo Tomtom! Helloooooo lickle Tomtom!'

giggled Daniel, waggling his fingers in the baby's face.

It was all very silly.

Of course, Kitty did like the new baby. He was very sweet, with his bald head, sticky-out ears, button nose and little, round, toothless mouth. But everybody made such a fuss of him, all the time, that Kitty felt quite left out.

She knew that was why she felt so strange, but knowing the reason didn't help. She wanted to be Mummy's baby, and that wasn't possible any more.

One day she went over to William's house to see if he wanted to play, but he and a boy from school called James were kicking a football around the garden. Kitty joined in for a while, but she soon felt bored. They didn't want her to play – she could tell. So, feeling left out, she came home.

Then she rang Rosie's house – and found out that Rosie had gone over to Anita's for the day.

Why didn't they ask me? Kitty thought – and felt even more left out.

What could you do when life seemed so flat? Kitty looked at all her toys and they bored her, even the castle that had once seemed so magical. Her paints were dirty, the fuzzy felts seemed babyish, her crayons needed sharpening, the Plasticine was all mixed up and she needed some new ...

What can I do? thought Kitty.

She heard Mum's voice and wandered across the landing to her room. Mum was bending over the changing pad, where a pair of little, fat, pink legs waved in the air. Baby Thomas had no clothes on. Kitty peered at him and giggled, because she felt a bit embarrassed.

'What is it?' asked Mum.

'He looks rude,' said Kitty.

'No he doesn't, he looks lovely,' said Mum, in that soppy voice, turning the baby over to powder his bottom. Kitty stared and didn't think he looked lovely at all.

She watched as Mum got the disposable nappy and its plastic cover, and started to put it on Tom. Then the little vest, then the blue all-in-one suit, then a little cardigan and a blue woolly bonnet with a bobble on the top.

'He looks like a fat parcel,' said Kitty, but Mum didn't hear.

'Who's my beautiful baby boy, then?' she whispered, cuddling Baby Thomas close.

'Mum – will you play with me?' whined Kitty.

'No, Kitty, I'm putting Tom in his pram in the garden and planting bulbs. Why don't you come out and help me?'

'Gardening's boring,' wailed Kitty. Mum shrugged and walked out, carrying the baby.

Later, looking down from her bedroom window, Kitty could have kicked herself. It would have been fun messing about in the soil with Mum. The sun was out, the baby was asleep in the pram, and Mum was bending over the flower-bed with a trowel in her hand. Kitty knew she could have made herself really dirty and not been told off.

But the bad Kitty had spoken, and now she couldn't go out and say sorry. She couldn't. When you've been bad you need a sort of excuse to be good again …

Kitty looked helplessly around her room and spotted Mr Tubs lying on the floor with his bottom in the air. Without thinking she picked him up and cuddled him close. Whenever she felt lonely and unhappy Mr Tubs was there. She could tell him everything, and he always gave her good advice. It's true! Inside her head Kitty always seemed to hear Mr Tubs talking and telling her what to do.

'Who's my beautiful bear then?' whispered Kitty, in a Mummy-type voice.

Mr Tubs looked cross and growled that he wasn't a baby.

'Oh yes you are! You're my baby,' said Kitty. 'Mr Tubs, you're so clever you're a genius!'

She took her teddy through to Mum's bedroom, and laid him down on the changing pad. Soon there was talcum powder all over his fur, but that didn't matter. It made him smell just like baby Tom … when his nappy was clean, of course!

It took longer than Kitty expected. The disposable nappy was easy, but it took a lot of fiddling to get the little vest on, as Mr Tubs was too fat. Then it took even longer to cram his tubby arms and legs into the red and white striped all-in-one suit. Then Kitty hunted around and found a clean white cardigan in Mum's baby drawer. She put some blue bootees on him for good measure. Finally she pulled a white bonnet over his ears – which stuck out under it like two lumps.

'Der! Whoo's mumma's ickle bearikins?' cooed Kitty.

Mr Tubs looked very funny – and very cross indeed. Kitty laughed and laughed as she picked him up in just the way Mum picked up Baby Thomas, with one hand under his bottom for support.

She opened the back door and walked out

into the garden, very slowly, as if she was
carrying a real child. Mum glanced up and for a
second she was taken in – since, from behind,
Mr Tubs looked like a lumpy little parcel of
baby, just like Tom.

'Who ...?' she began, looking puzzled.

Then Kitty got closer and turned him
round. Mum dropped her trowel, rocked back
on her heels and laughed as if she would burst.

'Can I put my baby in the pram too, Mum?' asked Kitty.

Mum got up, still laughing and took Mr Tubs from Kitty. 'What have you done? Oh, Kitsy,' she spluttered, 'I think your baby's even more beautiful than mine!'

They sat Mr Tubs in the bottom end of the pram, where Tom's feet didn't even reach. He looked very funny peering over the end, wearing the bonnet, and with talcum powder on his nose.

'I think they'll both sleep now,' said Mum, 'so shall you and I steal some time together, KittyKat?'

'Yes please, Mum,' beamed Kitty.

Extract from *I'm Bored!* by Bel Mooney, Mammoth

Dear Mum and Dad ...

Ian Whybrow

*Little Wolf has been sent to Cunning College to
learn his Uncle Bigbad's nine rules of badness.
Every day he writes home to his mum and dad
to tell them his news. In this letter we can see
that it does not take him long to discover Uncle
Bigbad's cunning tricks!*

Dear Mum and Dad,

No cleaning today, hooray! And guess what, I
have learned 2 Rules of Badness already!

I found a quite clean notebook in one of the
desks and I wrote in it.

Uncle came into the classroom. He was

shining up his big, gold BAD badge with his sleeve. I said, 'Hum ... nice! When will I get my badge?'

Uncle was nasty. He said, **'Not until you know the 9 Rules of Badness and that will take you years and years because you are not crafty enough to find them out swiftly.'**

I said, 'Maybe not, but I am still going to try my hardest.'

Uncle said, **'Very well, my clueless cub. Let us start with a story which might help you out. 2 Rules of Badness are hidden in it, but you are much too small and hopeless to find them!'**

I said, 'Never mind. Tell me the story anyway.'

So Uncle smiled his big horrible smile and he began.

'**Once upon a time there were 3 little piggies and they got on my nerves singing that they were not afraid of Bigbad Wolf. And they kept going "Ha-Ha-Ha-Ha-Ha-Ha" all the time. So I huffed and I huffed and I puffed their houses down and ate them.**'

I made a joke. I said, 'Gosh, Uncle, fancy eating their houses! Were the bricks tasty?'

Uncle said, '**Silence, Speck! That is not funny! GGGRRR! I once had a blasted dreadful accident with a brick house. I nearly blew my head off trying to huff it down. So you blinking blunking keep quiet about brick houses!**'

I said, 'Well, now I think I can make a guess. I know what Rules 1 and 2 are, Uncle! The answer is:

Rule 1. Huff and puff a lot.
Rule 2. Say loads of rude words,

Uncle got very
angle. He said,
**'GGGRRR! How
do you know
that? You must
have cheated!
Somebody told
you those rules!'**

I said, 'Nobody
told me. I guessed!' And I wrote Rules 1 and 2
in my Book of Badness.

RULE 1. HuFF AND PuFF A LOT.

RULE 2. SAy LoADS oF RuDE WORDS.

He went, **'GGGRRR!'** and bit a lump out of
the sink.

Love from

Littly

Extract from *Little Wolf's Book of Badness* by Ian
Whybrow, Collins

Collector Mania
Diana Hendry

Tess loved collecting things. From the time she was a baby, she had Collector Mania. At first people thought it was funny but eventually Mum got fed up with Tess and her collecting craze. Then Tess decided to collect the strangest thing of all!

I don't know where my sister Tess got the idea. Mum says she's a magpie, always collecting things. I think she's got Collector Mania. I think she was born with it.

It began with dummies. Yes, dummies! When she was a baby she had about a dozen of them hanging from her cot and pram. By the time she was four it was plugs. That was a really embarrassing one. You'd think plugs would be hard to collect. I mean we only have three in our house – the sink plug in the kitchen, the bath plug and the washbasin plug. That meant that Tess had to collect other people's plugs. Well, I'm being kind. She had to steal other people's plugs. Wherever we went, Tess would come home with a plug in her pocket.

Of course nobody called it stealing because Tess was only four. Four and strong enough to yank a plug off its chain! And she looked very sweet, my sister, with her hair in little ginger bunches and her nose all freckles. People thought it rather funny when she went off with their plug. At least they *said* they did. I don't suppose it really is funny if you're just about to have a bath and suddenly discover you don't have a plug.

Mum kept saying Tess
was too little to know any
better. But there was a
really good reason why Tess
liked plugs. She liked the
way the water went
whirling down the plug hole
when you pulled the plug
out. She could play with a
plug for hours, shouting,
'Whirly, Whirly, Whirly!
Twirly, Twirly, Twirly!'

There was no good
reason for the next craze –
the collection of boxes that
began to grow under her
bed. Matchboxes. Shoe
boxes. Cardboard boxes
that someone had packed a
present in at Christmas.
Big supermarket boxes.

Those boxes you get from the corner shop with Cox's Apple Pippin on the side and bumpy, purple paper at the bottom where the apples sit. Old, wooden boxes Tess bought from junk shops with her pocket money. Boxes covered with shells. Tin boxes with pictures on the lids. Tiny, velvet-lined boxes that had once held gold rings. Money boxes without any money in them. Oh, and egg boxes. Loads and loads of egg boxes.

In fact none of Tess's boxes had anything inside them.

'Tess,' I said to her when she was six, 'a box is for keeping things in.'

'I know, James,' Tess told me, with one of her scornful, I-am-not-an-idiot looks. 'But I like to think about what I *might* put in them.'

'I suppose you'll use them for whatever stupid thing you decide to collect next,' I said and I gave her look for look.

I wish I'd never said that. I saw her eyes suddenly brighten. I thought I'd better warn

Mum. 'She's thinking about what to collect
next,' I said.

Mum groaned. 'Let's hope it's small,' she
said. 'Do you think she might choose buttons or
bottle-tops this time?'

But buttons didn't appeal to Tess, nor did

bottle-tops. Stones did.

It's amazing how many different kinds of stones there are. And all sizes. Tess used to stagger home from school with a bag full of them. They weighed down the pockets of her jacket.

I quite liked the stones. Some of them had nice shapes. They were smooth or rough. You could nurse a smooth, round one in your pocket and that was rather nice.

They were all shades of grey, brown and black. Some of them had flecks of different colours. Some were like little chunks of marble. We broke one stone open and it had a milky middle.

Tess spent hours laying the stones out on her bedroom floor and then packing them into her boxes. She stuck labels on the boxes. Mum had to write them for her but Tess knew what they all were.

'Slate isn't really a stone,' I said to Tess.

'That's what you think,' said Tess.

'My teacher says it comes from rocks – from cliffs. There's quarries full of slate. So there!'

Actually I really liked the slate. It was so thin and fine and you could write on it in chalk. Mum said that once upon a time children used slates and chalk in school, instead of paper and pencils. I got Tess to give me a piece of slate as a swap for – you've guessed it – another box.

Anyway, it got to the point when Mum and I began to think that all those stones would fall through the floor of Tess's bedroom and into the living room below. We might even be killed one day by an avalanche of stones.

'ENOUGH IS ENOUGH!' Mum said very loudly and slowly, so we knew she meant it. 'You can choose your favourites and keep them in ONE box,' Mum said. 'The rest will have to go. And the boxes.'

I expected Tess to make an awful fuss. But she didn't. She was bored with boxes and stones. She'd got a new craze.

It wasn't long before Mum and I began to wish she'd stuck with the stones. Stamp collecting only lasted three weeks but we wished it had lasted longer. Or that someone could have talked her into collecting marbles or Pokémon cards. Anything! Anything!

Because what Tess decided to collect next was...a family!

Extract from *The Crazy Collector* by Diana Hendry, Barrington Stoke. Artwork by Annie West

The Turtle and the Crane
as told by Wendy Body

*People all over the world tell stories. Many
stories are about animals. This one is about the
friendship between a turtle and a crane. It is
told to children in the Far East.*

This is the story of Yim Sung, a poor Chinese
fisherman who had no wife, no money and no
food. He lived with his grumpy old mother in a
tiny cottage with tiny cherry trees by the sea.
They were both very unhappy.

'It's your fault we're hungry, Yim Sung,'

grumbled his mother. 'Why don't you go and catch some fish for us to eat?'

So the next day, Yim Sung went out in his boat to catch the biggest fish he could find. He hoped it would make his mother happy. But instead of catching a fish when he cast his net into the sea, he caught an enormous turtle.

'Thank goodness,' said Yim Sung. 'Now we will have lots to eat.'

Then he looked at the turtle and saw that it had tears in its big brown eyes.

'You poor thing,' said Yim Sung. 'I can see that you have troubles of your own. I will not harm you.'

So he let the turtle go and set sail for home.

But before he could reach the shore, a huge storm came and Yim Sung's boat sank beneath the waves. He found himself in the world at the bottom of the sea, with a beautiful princess.

Yim Sung noticed that her big brown eyes were filled with tears – just like the turtle he had set free.

'Yim Sung, please stay with me,' said the Princess. 'I am so lonely.' Yim Sung agreed to stay with her for three days.

It was lovely. They laughed, they sang and they danced. Yim Sung was very happy, but he knew he had to return to his mother (even though she would only tell him off for not catching any fish).

When he thought that three days had passed Yim Sung asked the Princess if he could leave her world. She agreed and gave him three tiny boxes. 'Only open them when you must,' she said.

When Yim Sung got back to his mother's cottage he saw that everything had changed. His mother had died and the tiny cherry trees had grown old and withered.

He had been away for over a hundred years.

'Now what shall I do?' sobbed Yim Sung and then he remembered the three boxes.

He opened the first box and out fell a crane's feather. He opened the second and a puff of white smoke came out.

He opened the third and saw a mirror – a mirror which showed him he had become an old man.

He sighed and said, 'I do wish I was back with the Princess.'

The next second the withered old cherry trees burst into blossom, the sun shone and Yim Sung had changed into a beautiful white crane.

A voice called out, 'Yim Sung, come down to the sea and dance with me!'

So Yim Sung went to the shore and saw the turtle with the big brown eyes. It was the Princess who had changed her shape again.

The turtle and the crane danced together … and they are dancing still.

The Turtle and the Crane as told by Wendy Body, from *Our Favourite Stories from Around the World*, Longman

A Day in the Life of a Killer Cat
Anne Fine

Ellie's cat Tuffy is always up to mischief. This week so far he has brought home a dead bird and a dead mouse. Poor Ellie cannot believe her eyes when she sees Tuffy's latest 'gift'! Read this entry from Tuffy's diary to find out what happened.

Thursday

Okay, Okay! I'll try and explain about the rabbit. For starters, I don't think anyone's given me enough credit for getting it through the cat-flap. That was not easy, I can tell you. It took about an hour to get that rabbit through

that little hole. That rabbit was downright fat. It was more like a pig than a rabbit, if you want my opinion.

Not that any of them cared what I thought. They were going mental.

'It's Thumper!' cried Ellie. 'It's next-door's Thumper!'

'Oh, Lordy!' said Ellie's father. 'Now we're in trouble. What are we going to do?'

Ellie's mother stared at me.

'How could a cat do that?' she asked. 'I mean, it's not like a tiny bird, or a mouse, or anything. That rabbit is the same size as Tuffy. They both weigh a ton.'

Nice. Very nice. This is my family, I'll have you know. Well, Ellie's family. But you take my point.

And Ellie, of course, freaked out. She went berserk.

'It's horrible,' she cried. 'Horrible. I can't believe that Tuffy could have done that. Thumper's been next door for years and years and years.'

Sure. Thumper was a friend. I knew him
well.

She turned on me.

'Tuffy! This is the end. That poor, poor
rabbit. Look at him!'

And Thumper did look a bit of a mess, I
admit it. I mean, most of it was only mud. And
a few grass stains, I suppose. And there were
quite a few bits of twig and stuff stuck in his
fur. And he had a streak of oil on one ear. But
no one gets dragged the whole way across a
garden, and through a hedge, and over another
garden, and through a freshly-oiled cat-flap,

and ends up looking as if they're just off to a party.

And Thumper didn't care what he looked like. He was dead.

The rest of them minded, though. They minded a lot.

'What are we going to do?'

'Oh, this is dreadful. Next-door will never speak to us again.'

'We must think of something.'

And they did. I have to say, it was a brilliant plan, by any standards. First, Ellie's father fetched the bucket again, and filled it with warm soapy water. (He gave me a bit of a look as he did this, trying to make me feel guilty for the fact that he'd had to dip his hands in the old Fairy Liquid twice in one week. I just gave him my old 'I-am-not-impressed' stare back.)

Then Ellie's mother dunked Thumper in the bucket and gave him a nice bubbly wash and a swill-about. The water turned a pretty nasty brown colour (all that mud). And then, glaring at me as if it were all my fault, they tipped it down the sink and began over again with fresh soap suds.

Ellie was snivelling, of course.

'Do stop that, Ellie,' her mother said. 'It's getting on my nerves. If you want to do something useful, go and fetch the hair-drier.'

So Ellie trailed upstairs, still bawling her eyes out.

I sat on the top of the dresser, and watched them.

They up-ended poor Thumper and dunked him again in the bucket. (Good job he wasn't his old self. He'd have hated all this washing.) And when the water finally ran clear, they pulled him out and drained him.

Then they plonked him on newspaper, and gave Ellie the hair-drier.

'There you go,' they said. 'Fluff him up nicely.'

Well, she got right into it, I can tell you. That Ellie could grow up to be a real hot-shot hairdresser, the way she fluffed him up. I have to say, I never saw Thumper look so nice before, and he lived in next-door's hutch for years and years, and I saw him every day.

'Hiya, Thump,' I'd sort of nod at him as I strolled over the lawn to check out what was left in the feeding bowls further down the avenue.

'Hi, Tuff,' he'd sort of twitch back. Yes, we were good mates. We were pals. And so it was really nice to see him looking so spruced up and smart when Ellie had finished with him.

He looked good.

'What now?' said Ellie's father.

Ellie's mum gave him a look – the sort of look she sometimes gives me, only nicer.

'Oh, no,' he said. 'Not me. Oh, no, no, no, no.'

'It's you or me,' she said. 'And I can't go, can I?'

'Why not?' he said. 'You're smaller than I am. You can crawl through the hedge easier.'

That's when I realised what they had in mind. But what could I say? What could I do to stop them? To explain? Nothing. I'm just a cat.

I sat and watched.

Extract from *The Diary of a Killer Cat* by Anne Fine, Puffin

A Perfect Fit!
Geraldine McCaughrean

Dad thinks the tree is too big.
Neil thinks his clothes are too big.
But Mum knows best! Or does she?

Dad said the tree in the back
garden was too big.

'The roots will damage the
house,' he said. 'The roots take
water away from the flowers.
It's too big.'

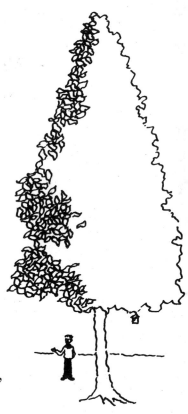

But Neil liked the
tree. In the mornings its
leaves cast a quivering
shadow-pattern on his bedroom
wall. What is more, it was the
ideal tree for a tree-house. Neil
had asked and asked to have a
tree-house. Mum said, 'Perhaps,
when you are bigger.'

But now that Dad had made up his mind the tree was too big, it looked as if the tree would be gone before Neil had time to get any bigger.

It was Saturday. Neil wanted to swing on the rope tied to a branch of the big old tree. It might be his last chance. But Mum wanted to take him to the shops.

'I am looking for a new wardrobe,' she said, 'and you need a new jumper.'

'Aaah, Mu-u-um!' groaned Neil.

He did not mean to sound ungrateful, but he and his mother could never agree about clothes.

Other mothers looked for the label in the neck of a shirt, read 6-7 years and said: 'Ah! This is perfect for my child, who is six (or seven).'

Not Neil's mum. She looked at the label and took out the shirt behind – the one marked 8-9 years. 'You need plenty of room to grow!' she would say.

Unfortunately, Neil never had time to grow into a shirt before she bought him another, two sizes bigger. All Neil's clothes were too big. They made him feel like a pea in an egg-cup.

They went to the shopping mall and tried on green jumpers and yellow jumpers, school jumpers and cricket jumpers.

'I like this,' said Neil, pretending to bowl a cricket ball.

'So do I,' said his mother. He could hardly believe it! The cricket jumper fitted him perfectly.

'I really, really like this,' Neil said, pretending to swing a cricket bat.

'So do I,' said Mum. She called the assistant. 'We will take this one ...' she said in her special shopping voice. (Could this really be true? Was she really going to buy Neil a jumper that fitted him?) '... if you have it in a bigger size.'

Neil did complain a bit, it's true.

'Too big,' he said, more than once. 'Too big, too big. **Toobigtoobigtoobig!**' But his mum only got cross and walked faster, so that Neil had to run to keep up. His sleeves flapped below his fingertips, ribbing rippled round his legs. Soon he had no more breath to say, 'Too big'. But he felt like a satsuma wearing an orange peel.

Mum led the way to the furniture store, to look at wardrobes. She looked at pine wardrobes and oak wardrobes, cheap and expensive wardrobes, old, modern and Swedish wardrobes. Sometimes when she opened the door, there was a mirror inside, and Neil saw himself, huge in his jumper. He looked like a cushion in a pillowcase.

'What do you think?' said his mother.

'Too big,' said Neil. Mum made a cross, gasping noise.

Some of the wardrobes had mirrors on the outside. Big white ghosts loomed up in the glass, and all of them were Neil in his cricket jumper.

'What do you think of this one?' said his mother.

'Too big,' said Neil.

Mum was so cross that she almost stamped.

'I'll take this one,' she said to the shop

assistant, so fiercely that he jumped backwards and fell over a bed.

'Too big! **Toobigtoobigtoobig!**' said Neil, until his mother rounded on him with a pointing finger.

'If you don't stop complaining about the jumper, Neil Willis, I shall stop your pocket money!'

'But I –' The boy in the mirror waved two sorrowful, dangling sleeve-ends in protest.

He looked like a lamb in sheep's clothing ...

The furniture store delivered the wardrobe on Friday. It came in a big van ...

... **too big** for the garden gate!

Extract from *Too Big!* by Geraldine McCaughrean, Corgi Pups.